P9-DCM-100

COLE:
NINJA
OF EARTH

By Greg Farshtey

SCHOLASTIC INC.
New York   Toronto   London   Auckland
Sydney   Mexico City   New Delhi   Hong Kong

If you purchased this book without a cover, you should be aware that this book is stolen property. It was reported as "unsold and destroyed" to the publisher, and neither the author nor the publisher has received any payment for this "stripped book."

No part of this publication may be reproduced in whole or in part, or stored in a retrieval system, or transmitted in any form or by any means, electronic, mechanical, photocopying, recording, or otherwise, without written permission of the publisher. For information regarding permission, write to Scholastic Inc., Attention: Permissions Department, 557 Broadway, New York, NY 10012.

ISBN 978-0-545-36993-0

LEGO, the LEGO logo, the Brick and Knob configurations and the Minifigure are trademarks of the LEGO Group. © 2012 The LEGO Group. Produced by Scholastic Inc. under license from the LEGO Group.
Published by Scholastic Inc. SCHOLASTIC and associated logos are trademarks and/or registered trademarks of Scholastic Inc.

12   15 16 17/0

Printed in the U.S.A.   40
First printing, January 2012

CONTENTS

FROM THE JOURNAL OF

Sensei Wu

Cole is the leader of my ninja team. I did not assign him this job. To do so would have been to force him into a role he might not have been right for, and to force the others to become followers. I allowed the true natures of the four youths to shine through. It became clear that Cole's nature is to take charge in any situation.

It fits, therefore, that he is my Ninja of Earth. Like the ground beneath our feet, he is solid and steady. He puts his friends first, preferring to focus on succeeding in the

mission than gaining personal glory. He did not join my team out of a need for revenge, like Kai; or curiosity, like Zane; or a need for adventure, like Jay. No, Cole became a ninja because it was the right thing to do.

Well, perhaps that was not the only reason.

When I first met Cole, he was climbing a mountain most felt could never be climbed. He was quite surprised to find me waiting for him at the top. As I talked with him, I learned that this was not the first time he had attempted something no one else could or would do. From sailing an unexplored ocean to skiing down an iceberg to hiking through trackless jungle, if it seemed impossible, Cole would try it. Yet, success brought no real satisfaction — it simply encouraged him to look for greater challenges.

Cole has many excellent qualities. He is strong, brave, smart, and disciplined. But he

4

lacked purpose. He was like a razor-sharp axe, with no tree to cut down. All the things he did to push himself to his limit served no other purpose than testing his endurance. Cole needed to know that all the things he could do, all his years of training, could in some way help others. I showed him that by learning to be a ninja and mastering Spinjitzu, he could be a part of saving this world.

How has he functioned as a leader? It has not been a simple task. His three partners are strong willed, unique people, each of whom is part of the team for his own reasons. Add to that the urgency of our mission and there has been very little time for anyone to get used to functioning as a team, let alone having a leader.

Cole has handled this situation well. He never announced that he would be leading the team, for he knew that would cause an argument. Instead, he simply took command

in the field as if it was the most natural thing in the world. In the heat of battle, there was no time for the others to dispute his role. Once it became obvious that his first priorities were the mission and the safety of his friends, the others started to accept his authority.

Still, there is a darker side to all this. Cole takes his position very seriously and worries that he will let his teammates down somehow. The night before a fight, Cole rarely sleeps, preferring to stay up and plan a strategy. He trains constantly. The standards he holds himself to are far higher than those he measures others against. Cole will not tolerate any weakness, hesitation, or failure on his part.

"These guys depend on me," he once told me. "If I freeze in battle, or I give the wrong order, or I haven't planned for every possibility, maybe someone gets hurt . . . or worse. That would put the mission in jeopardy, but

more than that, it would mean a friend was harmed because I wasn't smart enough or quick enough. I won't let that happen."

And so, I watch Cole with some concern. He drives himself harder than anyone I have ever known, and no man can do that for long. He will exhaust himself and that will not serve him or the team well. Even Earth will crumble if too much pressure is applied.

For now, Cole will continue on. He will try to keep Kai from charging blindly into danger. He will encourage Jay to put his inventive skills to good use. Zane may well remain a mystery to him, but Cole will try to make the Ninja of Ice feel part of the team. And just as they turn to Cole for guidance, I will try to remain someone he can go to for the same.

THE REAL
HERO

Oh, you have got to be kidding me," said Jay.

"Why would we have done such a thing as a joke?" asked Zane, honestly confused by Jay's reaction.

"We're wasting time," snapped Kai. "Get out of the way and I'll go."

"No, I'll go," said Jay. "You'll charge in and get into who knows what trouble."

"Personally," said Zane, "I think I am the logical choice to —"

"We'll all go," said Cole, steel in his voice. "**We're a team.** Time we started acting like it."

The four ninja stood on a high cliff over-looking a vast ocean. Dark clouds threatened overhead, **bolts of lightning** warning of the storm soon to come. The icy wind cut like a dagger and only Zane seemed to not feel a chill. That wasn't surprising, considering that one of Zane's hobbies was meditating at the bottom of half-frozen lakes.

The team had been successful so far, recovering two of the Four Weapons of Spinjitzu. Their quest had led them here in search of the Nunchuks of Lightning. But it wasn't the cliff or the storm or the cold that made them hesitate. It was the sight of an impossibly huge golden chain hanging in the air before their eyes. The links disappeared into the clouds far above.

There was only one way to find out where it led, and that was to climb. Cole wasn't worried about that. He was an experienced climber, after all. What concerned him was his team: Kai, always so quick to rush into

danger; Jay, constantly talking to cover his own fears; and Zane, so cold and humorless he almost seemed like he was from another planet. Each was brave and skilled, but each also wanted to be the hero on every mission. It was Cole's job to keep them working together, but it was far from easy.

Cole glanced back at Sensei Wu. The sensei nodded once. Cole turned to his team and said, "Let's go."

Leading the way, Cole began to climb. He had learned long ago not to look down or to think about how far one might fall. Doing either one would keep a person from getting very high. Behind him, the others climbed in silence.

It felt like hours had passed before Cole's head broke through the clouds and the climb was over. If the chain itself had been a startling sight, what the Ninja of Earth now saw was even more amazing. Before

his eyes were the ruins of an entire city—a *floating* city!

Cole pulled himself up and found his balance on an iron beam. The others quickly followed. "Wow," said Jay. "I wonder what the rent is like on this place."

"Fascinating," said Zane. "I have never seen anything like it. Who built it? How does it float in air? Does anyone still live here?"

"Can we save the questions?" said Kai. "The only thing that matters is the Nunchuks of Lightning. In case you've forgotten, Samukai and his skeleton crew have my sister as prisoner—and we know his warriors aren't very far behind us."

Kai took two quick steps along the beam. Suddenly, he lost his footing. Cole lunged and grabbed him before he could fall, pulling him back to safety.

"No one has forgotten anything," said Cole sharply. "But you won't do your sister any good by getting yourself hurt. Now let's search this place. The Weapon must be here somewhere."

"It would be faster if we split up," suggested Zane.

Cole shook his head. "Too dangerous, Zane, we don't know anything about this place. Now, move out, but be careful."

The ninja began to search. The city was ancient and looked like it had been abandoned for many centuries. The design of the buildings looked like nothing anyone had ever seen before, but now the structures were covered in dust and spider webs. That would not have been so bad, except—as Jay discovered, to his regret—the spiders were four feet wide with sixteen legs and **spat venom**.

There were no obvious clues as to who built the city, how, or why they left. There was no sign of any current occupants, other than the spiders, some birds, and other wildlife. Here and there were scattered bits of

rope, pieces of wood, fragments of cloth, and other items. Some of the buildings were almost completely intact, while others looked like they might fall down if anyone breathed too hard. All the while, lightning flashed overhead, as if the sky itself were angry at the trespassers in the city.

As the ninja moved farther into the city, Cole began noticing lightning symbols carved into the walls. At first, he thought they were just decoration. Then he realized that the bolts were pointing in various directions, almost like signs.

"That's it," Cole said. "The lightning carvings are pointing the way to the Nunchuks. All we have to do is follow them."

"Let's hope that's all they're pointing toward," said Jay.

The ninja moved swiftly through narrow, winding streets. At last, they reached a dead end. Before them was a vast

building made of what appeared to be marble. When Kai brushed against the stone, though, sparks flew and so did he. As he got up off the ground, he exclaimed, "What was that?"

"This is not any known type of building material," said Zane. "It's more like . . . **solid lightning** . . . but that makes no sense."

"If you expect things to make sense," chuckled Jay, "you're hanging around with the wrong people."

"We go in," said Cole. "Be careful not to touch the walls . . . and let's hope the floors aren't electrified, too."

Inside, the building was dark. Then a lightning bolt from above would suddenly illuminate it, the light streaming through holes in the roof. The floor was dirt and actually seemed to rise and fall beneath their feet. The interior walls crackled with electricity.

All four ninja could feel their hair standing on end from the energy in the air.

It was Cole who spotted the Nunchuks. They were hanging from a metal hook high upon the south wall. It didn't take a genius to know that **raw power** was flowing from the wall through the hook and if anyone touched either, it might be the last thing they ever did.

"I'll get it," said Jay. "I'm supposed to be the Ninja of Lightning, so . . ."

"No," said Cole. "Stay put. Zane, you know what to do."

Zane nodded and took a Shuriken out of his belt. He flung it at the east wall. It ricocheted off that to strike the north wall, then flashed to the west wall. Striking that, it shot for the south wall. The rotating blades sliced through the hook, and both hook and Nunchuks fell.

Jay took two steps, leaped, did a midair somersault, and caught the Weapon before

it hit the ground. He landed on his feet with a smile on his face. "Got it!"

The dirt floor suddenly heaved, knocking all four ninja off balance. Considering that the team had already run into an Earth Dragon and an Ice Dragon on their quest, Cole had a bad feeling he knew what was about to happen.

"Run!" he shouted.

Even as the ninja fled the building, a Lightning Dragon erupted from beneath the earthen floor. With a roar, it charged toward the ninja. Amazingly, it did no damage to the building. The solid "stones" of the structure turned ghostly, allowing the dragon to pass through as it pursued the heroes.

"The chain—head for the chain!" yelled Cole. Behind them, the dragon was breathing lightning bolts. One narrowly missed Cole, singeing his robe. "Kai, scout ahead, but **keep it quiet**!"

Kai moved with great stealth to the

place where the ninja had entered the city. He peered down the chain and saw armed skeleton warriors climbing up. Fortunately, they had not seen or heard him.

"We have company," he warned the other ninja.

"Great," said Jay. "Skeletons in front of us, Lightning Dragon in back—we're going to wind up sandwich meat."

Cole thought fast. "Maybe not," he said. "We just have to learn to fly."

Later, Kai, Jay, and Zane would tell Sensei Wu of their adventure while Cole secured the Nunchuks. It was the fastest job of inventing Jay had ever done. He lashed the pieces of wood together with the rope to form four frames shaped roughly like bird wings. Then he stretched the pieces of cloth across them to make crude hang gliders. Using these, the four ninja were able to escape the city with

the Nunchuks, soaring right past the enraged skeletons.

"So you were the hero," said the sensei.

Jay shook his head. "No, not me ... I mean, Zane was the one who threw the Shuriken so we could get the Weapon."

"Then Zane was the hero," said Sensei Wu.

"Well . . . Kai was the one who spotted the skeletons coming up the chain," said Zane. "If not for him, we might have climbed down into a trap."

Sensei Wu gave a slight smile. "I see. Kai was the hero, then."

Kai frowned. "No, that's not right, either. Maybe it was Cole? He suggested that Zane use his Shuriken, and that I scout for us, and that Jay come up with a way for us to fly out of there. Is that being a hero? He didn't really *do* anything . . . did he?"

Sensei Wu looked at the ninja. "Young ones, from what you have told me, Cole let the three of you use your skills to do what

21

you do best, rather than trying to do everything himself. Sometimes, the real hero is the
one who lets others be heroes."

Kai, Jay, and Zane would think about that
for a long time.

THE PHANTOM
NINJA

CHAPTER 1

Cole crouched at the edge of the cliff, peering down at the skeleton camp far below. Only two skeleton warriors were posted as guards this night. The rest were sleeping, no doubt dreaming of raiding villages and frightening innocent people. Before the night was over, they would be awakened to a far worse reality.

Jay, Zane, and Kai flanked Cole. Each of the four ninja had his own ideas of how to attack the skeletons. However, despite those different opinions, they had learned to work together as a team. Sensei Wu had made

25

Cole the leader, a responsibility he took extremely seriously. He had to, for it was far from an easy job.

"What are we waiting for?" Kai said in a fierce whisper. "Let's go down there and **smash them**."

"We might be able to capture the lot of them and make them talk," offered Jay. "I have a new invention made just for bagging skeleton warriors."

"Impractical," Zane replied. "We have no cage in which to hold them. Far better to beat them and drive them off. Perhaps they will lead us to their headquarters in this region."

"Quiet," Cole said. "We have a plan in place. We attack from the south and herd them toward the river. One of us will spring the trap that's set there and catch one skeleton that we can try to get answers from, if any of those boneheads knows anything . . . which I doubt."

"I don't remember voting for that plan," Kai answered. "Driving them away just means they come back again later. Spinjitzu 'em into a pile of pieces and you won't have any trouble from them anymore."

Cole closed his eyes for a moment and took a deep breath. When he opened them, he looked right at Kai and said, "You are still relatively new to this team, so I will remind you how we do things. I come up with the plan and we follow it as best we can. That's to keep the three of you safe and to make sure no innocent people get hurt in our fights."

"Cole is correct," said Zane. "But it may be that someone else would be better suited to map out our strategy. It is something to consider."

Cole pointed down below. "Let's debate after the battle. Jay, you use your flying harness to distract the guards. Zane and I will mount the attack. Kai, you head to the

river and make sure one ends up in the trap."

Kai shook his head. "Change of plan," he said. An instant later, he had run off into the darkness.

CHAPTER 2

Cole wanted to call after him, but the noise would wake the skeletons. He turned back to Zane and Jay, only to find Jay was gone, too. "Where did he go?" he asked Zane.

"I assume he wished to try out his new invention before Kai 'messes things up,'" replied Zane. "I suppose they saw flaws in your plan."

"Those two," Cole began, then stopped. There was no time to be angry. Kai and Jay were putting themselves in danger. "Let's go, Zane, we have to stop them."

But Zane was gone, too.

"All right, I'll do it myself," muttered Cole.

He was about to head down the mountain when he saw a **bright flash** from below. In the sudden illumination, he could see Jay holding a large contraption that was designed to shoot lightning bolts. Unfortunately, it had shot its bolt in the wrong direction. With a startled cry, Jay went flying through the air. He crashed hard into some trees.

The light and the noise awoke all the skeletons, just as Kai charged in. Now, instead of facing two guards, he was up against a dozen. Cole knew there was no time to waste. He dashed down the winding trail that led to the camp.

By the time he got there, Kai was in the midst of battle. Cole's eyes took in the whole scene, including the skeleton warrior about to strike Kai from behind. Cole launched himself into the air, intending to bring down the skeleton with a leaping kick. But before

he could land his blow, there was a harsh cracking sound off to his right.

Cole couldn't help but flick his eyes in that direction. To his horror, he saw a huge tree falling right toward him. Using all his agility, he twisted his body in midair and managed to stop his leap. He landed awkwardly on the ground and the tree followed right after, crashing into the camp just a few feet from him.

Kai was shouting in frustration. The falling tree had cut him off from his foes. Now the skeletons were fleeing toward the river. As he got to his feet, Cole spotted Zane emerging from the woods. One look at the young ninja's face told Cole that Zane had been responsible for knocking down the tree.

"This is great," Cole snapped as he helped the dazed Jay to his feet. "Well, we won't be catching any skeletons since no one was there to spring the trap. What kind of teamwork do you call that?"

"It was a stupid plan anyway," grumbled Kai. "If we had all hit them together, we could have taken the whole camp."

"Or if my invention had worked," Jay said.

"Had the tree landed six inches to the right, it would have disabled at least half the skeletons," Zane said.

Cole didn't answer. Instead, he just turned around and headed back to the ninja camp. He never looked back to see if the others were following.

CHAPTER 3

The next morning, Cole called a meeting. Sensei Wu was off meditating, so it seemed like a good time to talk to the other ninja.

"Things like last night can't happen again," he began. "Next time, someone might get killed. I'm the leader of this team, and—"

"Maybe that's the problem," Kai broke in. "Maybe we need a new leader."

"Could be, um, Kai is right," said Jay.

"I'm glad you agree with me," Kai replied, slapping Jay on the back. "Now, when I'm running things—"

"You?" Jay interrupted. "I was talking

about me. I think we need a leader who's more inventive. You kind of think with your fists."

Now it was Zane's turn to cut in. "Actually, I believe the team would benefit from a more analytical approach to things. Rushing into battle in the grip of fury is a **recipe for disaster**."

Cole abruptly stood up. "Okay. I've had it. You think it's easy leading the three of you? It's not. If one of you thinks you can do a better job, then go ahead."

With that, Cole walked away.

For a few moments, the three remaining ninja sat in uncomfortable silence. Zane was about to suggest they go after Cole when Kai spoke up.

"All right then," said the Ninja of Fire. "If that's how he feels, fine. Let's pick a new team leader."

"Okay," said Jay. "How? Should we ask Sensei Wu who should do it?"

"The sensei chose Cole," replied Zane. "It is logical that he would prefer to continue with him."

"We'll take a vote," said Kai. "The winner will be the new leader. We can even do a secret ballot."

Zane went and got three small pieces of paper and pencils. Each of the ninja wrote down a name, folded his paper, and then tossed it onto the ground in front of them. Kai did a quick shuffle of the papers. He picked them up and began to unfold the first.

"Okay, let's see who won and why I did," he said. Kai looked down at the first piece of paper and smiled as he said, "Kai."

He unfolded the second paper and his face fell. The others could see it had the name "Zane" written on it. The third paper turned out to be a vote for Jay.

"It would appear we all voted for ourselves," said Zane.

"Now what?" asked Jay.

Kai stood up. "The next mission we tackle will decide it," he said. "Whoever does the best job will be the new leader. So you guys better get some sleep tonight—you're going to need it."

ay was the first to wake up the next morning. Before he had even opened his eyes, he noticed that it felt unusually cold. He went to pull his blanket up, but his hand found nothing. Puzzled, he lifted one eyelid and took a look. His blanket was gone.

As he sat up, Jay wondered if some animal had snuck into camp during the night and dragged off the blanket. A quick glance showed him it would have had to be a bunch of animals, and very strong ones, too. Everything in the camp—the pots and pans, the weapons, the blankets, even the

wagon—was gone. The ninja had been robbed in the night.

Jay woke up Zane and Kai. Cole had been on guard duty last night, and if something like this had happened, then something worse might have happened to Cole. Together, the three ninja headed for the outskirts of the camp.

They found Cole in the tall grass. He was unconscious, but a little cold water revived him. He winced in pain as he opened his eyes and saw his three teammates.

"Ohhh, my head is pounding," said Cole. "What happened?"

"That's what we were going to ask you," said Jay. "Did someone hit you? I don't see any marks."

With some help from the others, Cole got to his feet. "I guess so. One minute I was keeping watch, the next, **bam!** I never saw or heard anyone, though. Are you guys okay?"

"Yes, but all our gear has been stolen," said Zane. "This makes no sense. If it was a skeleton warrior, would he not have harmed us rather than just taken our equipment?"

Cole shook his head. "I would have heard one of those boneheads from a mile off. I don't think this was any skeleton."

Kai noticed something buried in the tree bark next to him. Cautiously, he plucked a shuriken out of the wood. Attached to it was a note.

Kai unfolded it and read:

This is your first warning. I have taken your possessions and next I will take something much more precious from you. Your only hope is to surrender to me.
—The Phantom Ninja

Cole pulled his ninja hood off and ran his hand through his hair. "This is bad," he said. "This is very bad."

"Do you know this person?" asked Zane.

Cole shook his head. "Not personally, just by reputation. Before Sensei Wu approached any of us, he recruited an established ninja . . . or tried to. This warrior demanded gold in return for his services. When Sensei Wu said no, the Phantom Ninja didn't take it well. He vowed that Sensei would someday regret his decision . . . and it looks like today is the day."

"What are we so worried about? He's just one ninja. There are four of us. We can take him," Kai said.

"Not without a plan. Remember, it would seem he has far more experience than we do," said Zane.

Kai shrugged. "Okay, fine. So we need a plan. Who's going to make it?"

Jay folded his arms across his chest and leaned against the tree. "Well, Kai, that's usually the leader's job, isn't it?"

Almost by reflex, everyone turned to look

at Cole. He, in turn, took a couple of steps back. "Oh, no," he said. "I'm not in charge anymore, remember? One of you can do it this time . . . if you can decide who gets the honor."

Kai started walking away, beckoning for Zane and Jay to follow. "Forget it. We'll come up with a plan on our own."

Cole watched them go, a faint smile curling around the edges of his lips.

CHAPTER 5

When the ninja team reassembled a few hours later, Kai's group had the beginnings of a plan. Since there was no way to track the Phantom Ninja down, it would be necessary to lure him into a trap. Jay would act as bait in the camp, while the other ninja hid in the woods and waited to ambush their foe as soon as he showed himself.

"What if he spots the trap?" asked Cole.

"He won't," Kai replied. "Hey, we're ninja, aren't we?"

"So is he," Cole reminded the group.

As the sun set, Kai, Zane, and Cole took up positions in the woods. Jay busied himself puttering around the camp, trying to look like he wasn't waiting to be attacked. The hours dragged by. At one point, Zane almost **launched an attack** on a figure in the forest, only to discover it was a wild boar hunting for its dinner.

By midnight, even Kai was ready to admit that the trap had been a failure. Either the Phantom Ninja had spotted it, or he simply wasn't out prowling tonight. Kai started down the tree and was about to call out to the others to go back to camp when he heard Cole yelling. He couldn't make out the words, and the sound was cut off a moment later. But Kai knew where Cole had been posted and ran in that direction.

By the time he reached the spot, Cole was gone. All that remained was his black ninja hood, pinned to a tree with a dagger. A note was wrapped around the knife handle.

Zane and Jay arrived just as Kai was opening the note. By the light of Jay's torch, they read:

Sensei Wu is even more of a fool than I thought. Did you really think you could trap me with such an obvious trick? Now I am insulted. I have taken your friend Cole. Find him by the next day, and you can have him back. Otherwise, you will never see Cole again. Your first clue is to look where moss grows.

I am waiting for you.

— The Phantom Ninja

"We must find Sensei Wu," said Zane. "He must be informed."

"Right," snapped Kai. "And when he finds out why it happened, we'll be packing to go back home. No, we have to solve it ourselves. So let's think about the

first clue: 'look where moss grows.' Any suggestions?"

"Trees?" offered Jay. "We're in a forest, maybe he is trying to tell us Cole is still nearby."

Zane frowned. "Too obvious. As a clue, that would tell us nothing at all."

"Moss grows on trees. We're surrounded by trees," Kai said. "Doesn't give us much of a direction."

Zane's expression suddenly brightened. "Direction? Kai, I think you have figured out the clue."

"I did?"

"Where does moss grow? Moss grows on the *north* side of trees," said Zane. "That means he's taken Cole somewhere to the north of here."

"All right, here's what we do —" Kai began.

"Wait a minute," Jay interrupted. "It was your idea to make a trap for the Phantom

Ninja, and look what happened. Now we'll try things my way."

Kai wheeled on Jay, with **anger flashing** on his features. "And what way is that?"

"I can build something that can track the Phantom Ninja. Just give me some time, and —"

Zane cut him off. "Time is not something we have, Jay. What is needed is the same kind of analysis I just used to decode the clue."

"You said *I* figured out the clue!" said Kai.

Zane nodded. "You provided a direction, quite unknowingly, but it was my knowledge of the forest that —"

"Enough!" yelled Jay. The other two ninja turned to look at him. "We only have a day to find Cole. Let's not waste it arguing. We'll head north, and when we find him, we can each come up with our own plan to save him. Okay?"

Zane and Kai nodded their agreement. Together, the three ninja set off in silence into the north woods. Although they were a team, they had never felt less like one. Yet no one wanted to be the first to admit it.

CHAPTER 6

After walking for about an hour, they came to a bridge over a raging river. The timbers in the center of the span had been **smashed**, making it impossible to pass. A note was pinned with a ninja sword to the railing of the wrecked bridge. It read:

The three of you must find a way to make it across without using Spinjitzu, or Cole will not be making it back.

— The Phantom Ninja

"We can swim it," said Zane, then added, "I think."

"Says the guy who thinks sitting at the bottom of ice-cold ponds is fun," replied Jay. "If I only had my tools and some materials . . ."

Kai looked around. To his surprise, he spotted a length of rope nearby. Not far away was some of Jay's gear. "All right, this will be easy," he said. "All I have to do is tie the rope to one of those tree limbs overhead and swing across."

Jay, poring through his gear, ignored Kai. "Great, great. With all this, I can build rocket packs and we can fly across the bridge. Piece of cake."

Zane watched the two of them, his brow knitted with concern. Then he walked over to the nearest tree and held up his torch. Looking up, he shook his head. "Kai, these tree branches are rotten. In fact, all the big branches around here are. If you try to swing

from one, it will snap and you will wind up in the river."

"I can do it," insisted Kai.

"No. You can't," Zane replied. "The amount of momentum you would need to cross the river would make it almost certain the tree branch would break."

Jay walked over, his arms full of metal parts. "We don't need him to swing any-where. It won't take me long to build the rocket packs. Isn't it kind of funny how the Phantom Ninja just dropped my gear here?"

"I don't think it was meant to be funny," said Zane. "Not at all."

Jay set to work as Kai scaled the larg-est of the nearby trees. Zane watched as Kai shimmied out onto one of the branches and started tying the rope to it. Once he was done, he climbed down the tree and gave the rope a tug.

"Kai . . ." Zane began.

"I know what I'm doing!" snapped the Ninja of Fire.

Before Zane could say anything else, Kai stood up, took the rope in both hands, and leaped into space. He soared in a beautiful arc toward the river. At the apex of his swing, there was a sound like a **huge firecracker** going off. The next instant, arms flailing, Kai was falling toward the river.

Zane took three quick steps and leaped, hoping he had calculated Kai's rate of fall correctly. He caught his teammate in mid-air and used Kai's weight to propel them into a somersault. Zane landed on the remains of the bridge, each foot precariously balanced on opposite sides of a broken railing.

"You," Zane said, calmly but breathlessly, "have put on weight."

"Put me down," said Kai, his face almost as red as his ninja garb.

"If I do, you will get wet," Zane pointed out. "I have a better idea."

With one smooth motion, Zane hurled Kai backward toward the river bank. The Ninja of Fire landed in the dirt with a grunt. Jay burst out laughing at the sight, but the look on Kai's face quickly silenced him.

"How are you progressing, Jay?" asked Zane.

Jay shrugged. "Well . . . I can build a rocket pack, but only one. There aren't enough parts here for two others. So one of us could use it to get across, but that's all."

"You go ahead, then," said Kai, back on his feet and brushing the dirt off his clothes "Find Cole. Zane and I will manage to get across somehow and catch up to you."

Jay hesitated for a moment, then he strapped on his rocket pack. He was just about to fire it up when Zane said, "Wait! We're making a mistake."

"Another one?" said Jay.

"Remember the note," Zane explained. "It said the *three* of us must find a way across the river . . . not just one. If you go over the river and we stay here, we will have failed the test, and who knows what will happen to Cole? No, we must find a way to succeed together."

Kai kicked the rope that lay on the ground. "Rope won't do us much good if the tree branches aren't strong enough to hold us."

"And Jay is not strong enough to carry both of us across," said Zane. "But we cannot just give up. There must be a way."

Jay suddenly smiled and rushed over to where Kai stood. "I think maybe there is. Quick, tie the end of the rope around your waist, Kai."

"Huh?" said Kai, but then did as he was asked. "What crazy idea do you have now?"

"Now you, Zane," said Jay, offering his friend the rope. "Tie it around you. I don't know why I didn't think of this before."

Once Kai and Zane both had the rope securely knotted around their waists, Jay took the free end of it and tied it around himself. Kai still looked puzzled, saying, "Great. Time's running out and he wants to experiment with our lives."

"No, no," said Zane. "I believe I see his idea. It will turn out to be a very good one . . . if we survive it."

"Thanks. I think," said Jay. "Now, hang on as tight as you can!"

With that, Jay fired up his rocket pack. The thrust of the engine propelled him forward toward the river. Behind him, the rope pulled tight and Kai and Zane found themselves being jerked off their feet and into the air.

"Oh, boy," yelled Kai. "How do I get off this ride?"

Zane's answer was cut off as both he and Kai realized that the other side of the cliff was fast approaching.

"Tell me you know how to land, please!" shouted Zane.

"Well, actually . . ." Jay yelled back.

As he passed over the far bank, Jay abruptly cut the power to the rocket pack. He went into a nosedive, slamming into a bunch of prickly bushes along with Zane and Kai.

"If you ever—ow!—come up with an idea like that again—**ouch!**—you won't just have the Phantom Ninja to worry about!" threatened Kai, as he pulled thorns out of his arms and legs.

"Now, Kai," Zane said gently. "The idea *did* work, and that is what counts. We made it across the river and met the Phantom's condition. Now we should—"

An arrow shot past Zane and buried itself in a nearby tree. Wrapped around the shaft was another note.

"Never mind the arrow!" shouted Kai, already on the run. "He had to be close enough to shoot it! Find him!"

The three ninja charged into the forest. They were so focused on the chase that none of them noticed the vines stretched across the path. In short order, all three had sprung traps and were hanging upside down from tree limbs high in the air.

"I think you left out the part about 'watch where you're going,'" Jay said to Kai.

"Look below!" cried Zane.

Down in the clearing stood a ninja, clad from head to toe in charcoal gray. He was looking up at his three captives and laughing. "Is this what Sensei Wu has taught you?" said the Phantom Ninja. "I suppose I must have overrated him as a ninja master."

"Just cut us down," growled Kai, "and I'll show you a few things the sensei has taught us."

"You will get yourselves down, I'm sure, hothead," the Phantom Ninja said. "But here's a clue to think about while you are up there: A man is drowning, yet not wet. Where is he?"

Before any of the ninja could answer, their nemesis had vanished back into the forest. Kai immediately began to swing back and forth on his vine until he built up enough momentum to swing his arms up toward his ankles. He grabbed the vine with one hand and with the other tore his foot loose from it. Then, he swung over to the others and repeated the process for them. After that, it was a long drop to the ground, but Sensei Wu had taught them all how to fall safely.

"When I catch up to that guy, I swear—" Kai began.

"Save it," said Jay. "That 'man drowning' is probably Cole, which means we better figure out that clue fast."

"But in what can a man drown without getting wet?" wondered Zane. "On the face of it, it does not seem to make sense."

"You can drown in sorrow," Kai said, already heading north again. The others followed along behind. "You can drown in debt."

"Somehow, I don't think Cole borrowed money from the Phantom Ninja," Jay said.

"You can drown in other things," Zane said grimly. "Grain. Dirt. Sand."

Kai turned to look at Zane. "Sand? Wait a minute, didn't Sensei Wu say something about a big patch of sand somewhere nearby?"

"No," said Jay. "I think he said *quick*sand!"

"That's it!" shouted Kai, racing through the forest now. "It has to be!"

They had gone only a few hundred yards when they came to a clearing. About one hundred feet from where they stood was a large pool of quicksand, with a black-garbed figure half-submerged in it. The figure was motionless, no doubt trying to keep from moving too much to slow the rate of sinking.

"Cole!" yelled Jay. "We're here! **Hang on!**"

The figure in the quicksand didn't answer. *Or he can't*, thought Kai.

Jay rushed forward to save his friend. But he didn't notice the vine stretched across

his path. Fortunately for him, Kai's keen eyes spotted the danger. The Ninja of Fire leaped, bringing Jay down with a flying tackle. They fell on the vine, which triggered a hail of daggers from a nearby stand of trees. The knives whistled over the heads of the two ninja.

"You saved my life," said Jay.

Kai got up off the ground. "You were acting like me, rushing in without thinking," he said, smiling. "And only I'm allowed to act like me in this team." Kai bent down and ripped the vine free. "Now let me see if I can put this to use."

Twirling the vine over his head like a lasso, Kai threw it toward the figure in the quicksand. The end of the vine landed right in the center of the pool, but the intended target made no move to grab it. "Cole, take hold of the vine and we'll pull you out!" Kai shouted.

No response.

"Do you think perhaps he is already . . . ?" asked Zane.

Kai abruptly turned around and started walking back into the woods. "If he doesn't want to be rescued, then we shouldn't waste our time. Let's go."

"Wait a minute!" Jay exploded. "You can't just leave him to die."

"Sure, I can," said Kai.

Zane started walking away as well. "It seems the most logical thing to do."

"You're both crazy!"

Kai's voice dropped to a whisper. "Jay, shut up and start walking. Trust me."

Jay turned back to look at the pool of quicksand. He was sure the figure had sunk lower in the last few moments. How could they just leave Cole behind? But Kai and Zane seemed certain of their actions. Slowly, he started to follow them.

Their journey was halted by an axe that flew through the air and struck the ground right at Kai's feet. The three looked up to see the Phantom Ninja standing in a tree.

"Just abandoned him to die, hmmm?" he said. "What will Sensei Wu say about that?"

"We didn't abandon anyone," said Kai. "It was a dummy in that pool. Which only seems fair since all three of us are dummies, too. Right?"

"If you say so," replied the Phantom Ninja.

"First, you attack Cole and knock him out, but you don't leave a mark," said Kai. "That takes a lot of skill. I don't think even Sensei Wu could do that."

"Then, when Kai, Cole, and I were hiding in the woods, you chose Cole as your hostage," said Zane. "One has to wonder why."

"Oh, no," said Jay. "You're not saying . . . ?"

"Yes," said the Phantom Ninja. "They are." He pulled off his hood to reveal Cole's face.

"You!" exclaimed Jay.

"Him," said Kai. "Now the question is, why?"

"Simple," said Cole, as he made his way down the tree. "The three of you were questioning my leadership. Each of you thought

you'd been passed over for the job for some reason. I wanted to show you that isn't true."

Cole reached the ground and walked over to them. "Zane, you had the knowledge to figure out the moss clue. Jay, you created the invention that got the team across the river. Kai, your combat skill helped you spot the trap I set, as I knew it would. All three of you have unique abilities, and you know what you can do well . . . and all three passed the challenges I expected you to."

"I think I see," said Zane. "The true role of a leader is not only to know what he does well, but to know what all the members of his team do well. Thus you know how best to employ them on a mission."

"Exactly," said Cole.

"So all that stuff about the Phantom Ninja," said Kai, "you made all that up."

Cole hesitated a moment before answering. "Well, no. I wish I had. But there really is a Phantom Ninja. He really did ask for

money to help the sensei and was turned down. But so far his **VOWS of vengeance** are just talk."

"That's a relief," said Jay. "Between Garmadon, Samukai, and the skeleton warriors, we have enough enemies to worry about. But here's the really important question: Where's our stuff?"

Cole laughed. "Back in camp. I snuck back and returned it after you left."

"We should head there, then," said Zane. "It seems we have a lot to discuss."

CHAPTER 8

The journey back to the camp was made in silence. As they entered the clearing, Cole stopped, stunned. Not only was all the gear gone from camp—again—but the campsite itself was **completely trashed**.

"Very funny, Cole," snapped Kai.

"Really, this is carrying the game too far," commented Zane.

"Wait a minute, I didn't do this," insisted Cole. "When I saw it last, the camp was intact. Someone else must have come here after I left."

"Correct," a harsh voice replied. "And that someone was me."

The four ninja turned at the same time to see another ninja. This one was garbed in charcoal gray and standing at the edge of the clearing. None of them had any doubt who he was, but they still felt a surge of disbelief. After all, how could it be?

"The Phantom Ninja?" said Jay. "You have to be kidding me."

Faster than the eye could follow, the Phantom Ninja hurled two shuriken. They hit Jay just above the shoulders, pinning the fabric of his ninja outfit to a tree.

"Does that look like a joke to you?" asked the Phantom Ninja.

"What do you want here?" demanded Cole.

"I heard someone was using my name in vain." The Phantom Ninja chuckled. "It seemed a good time to come and ask for payment. I have already taken your weapons

66

and your campsite. What else do you have that might be of value?"

Jay yanked the shurikens out of the tree. The other three ninja spread out, each ready for combat. "I think we can find something to give you," said Kai. "But you might not like it."

The Phantom Ninja leaped high in the air from a standing start, did a midair somersault, and landed on his feet in front of Kai. "Do your worst, boy."

Kai unleashed a hail of punches and kicks. The Phantom Ninja blocked all of them without even breaking a sweat. Then, spotting an opening in Kai's defenses, he landed a **sparrow strike** in Kai's midsection that left the young ninja gasping for breath.

"You have power, but no technique," said the Phantom Ninja. "You won't live long in this business."

"It is not a business to us," said Zane, closing in. "It is a duty."

This time, it was the Phantom Ninja's turn to attack. But every blow was parried by Zane with ease. Finally, the Phantom Ninja stopped and took a step back, his eyes crinkling up as he smiled beneath his hood.

"Now, you're interesting," said the warrior. "Maybe more than you know. Observant . . . I like that."

Zane said nothing. He saw no reason to inform the Phantom Ninja that he had noticed a pattern in his combat style. Whenever his opponent was about to strike with his left hand, he would drop his right shoulder a quarter of an inch. Noticing that had allowed Zane to anticipate and block his moves.

"Shall we try it again?" asked the Phantom Ninja.

"Repeating the same action and expecting a different result is the definition of insanity," answered Zane, nonetheless preparing for another round of fighting.

The Phantom Ninja took a step forward,

dropping his right shoulder. Zane prepared for a blow from his enemy's left hand. Instead, the Phantom Ninja **lashed out** with his right, felling Zane with one strike.

"No," said the Phantom Ninja, looking down at his opponent. "Insanity was thinking you could beat me."

Cole began to whirl around, using the power of Spinjitzu to transform into a tornado. "Come on, Jay. I've had enough of this guy."

Jay nodded, hurling the two shuriken even as he channeled his Spinjitzu power into an electrical whirlwind. The Phantom Ninja blocked the missiles with little effort. Cole and Jay headed for their foe from opposite directions, intending to trap him between them. But to their surprise, the Phantom Ninja also transformed into a whirlwind, rotating just as fast as they were, but in the opposite direction. When they came close, the force of his cyclone overwhelmed theirs and they were sent sprawling on the ground.

"You . . . you know Spinjitzu, too?" said Jay, stunned.

"I know a lot of things. This, for example," said the Phantom Ninja. In the next instant, he had completely disappeared.

Cole sprang to his feet. "Where did he go?"

"I don't know," said Jay, joining him. "I never saw him move."

Zane and Kai were back in the fight as well, though now there was no one to battle. "Invisibility would make an already difficult opponent . . . **unstoppable**," said Zane.

"No one is unstoppable," said Cole. "He didn't leave us any weapons, but we'll make do with what we have. Grab sticks, rocks, anything. Throw them at the spot where you last saw him."

The ninja readied their makeshift weapons. Just before they were about to throw, the Phantom Ninja reappeared right where

he had been before. He took off his hood and smiled at the young men. "Well, now I see why that one is the leader. He thinks on his feet."

"Interesting illusion," said Zane. "How did you manage that?"

"Oh, it's no illusion . . . not really, not the way you mean. I simply empty my mind of all thought. In effect, I cease to exist mentally. And with no mind, no awareness of self, I disappear," the Phantom Ninja replied.

All four ninja moved in to attack. As the Phantom Ninja fended them off with little effort, he caught Jay in the midst of a flying kick and hurled him over his shoulder. "You guys should have no problem learning that one," he continued. "Emptying your minds should be a cinch for you."

Cole looked around. The other three ninja were exhausted, but continuing to fight. Their opponent was fresh and didn't even seem to be straining. At the same time, the Phantom

Ninja did not seem to be really trying to beat them so much as looking to see what they could do. One way or the other, this fight had to end soon, Cole knew. Otherwise, his team would collapse and anything might happen.

His plan was risky, but it was the only thing left to try. "Close in!" he yelled. "Don't give him room to move!"

The Phantom Ninja made no extra effort to counter as the four advanced on him. Even as they were coming at him from every side, he simply blocked their blows as he had been doing all along.

Cole waited until he and his team were almost on top of the Phantom Ninja and each other before they shouted, **"Spinjitzu! Now!"**

Before the Phantom Ninja could react, all four ninja transformed into living tornadoes. It was perhaps the most dangerous thing they had ever done, invoking the power of Spinjitzu when they were so close together.

But it was working. The force of their spinning lifted the Phantom Ninja high into the air, and kept him helpless.

Cole waited for one minute, then two, until he was sure the Phantom Ninja must be defeated. Then he signaled the others to cease their spinning. Deprived of the air pressure that was keeping him aloft, the Phantom Ninja slammed into the ground . . . and laughed, and laughed.

Cole's heart sank. Was the Phantom Ninja still ready to fight? If so, then what?

But the fallen foe made no effort to get up and attack. Instead, his laughs subsided into warm chuckles and he grinned at Cole. "I guess I lose my wager."

"Wager?" said Cole. "What wager?"

"Sensei Wu and I made a little bet. He told me about some of the tension in camp. I wagered that, even in a crisis, his team would be too fractured to follow their leader. But you four proved me wrong."

"Wait a minute," yelled Kai. "You know Sensei Wu well enough to make bets with him? I thought you two were **bitter enemies**!"

The Phantom Ninja sat up. "Oh, that's just the story we agreed to tell. See, I was a bandit, way back when, until Wu caught me. Instead of taking me to jail, he made a deal with me. I would restrict my activities to robbing other criminals, and pass any information I learned about major threats to him."

"So all this . . . ?" said Cole.

". . . was to give you guys a common enemy when you needed one," said the Phantom Ninja. "You all want to defeat the skeletons, but you have different plans of attack. That's why you aren't working well together. With me, there was no time for arguing about the best plan of action. And look what happened."

Zane helped the Phantom Ninja to his feet. "Now what?" asked the Ninja of Ice. "You ambush us, batter us, and we are supposed

to let you go free and continue a life of theft and banditry?"

The Phantom Ninja clapped Zane on the back. "That's the score, kid—unless, of course, you want to try and defeat me a second time. But I'm not sure I'd advise that."

"Why, you . . ." Kai began, taking a forceful step toward the Phantom Ninja.

"Kai, stop!" snapped Cole. "We'll take him at his word . . . for now. If we discover that he's lying to us about anything, we'll find him again. And now he knows that we can beat him."

The Phantom Ninja smiled and shook his head. "Oh, come on . . . you don't think I would be ready for that trick the next time?"

Cole walked up to his opponent, stopping when he was nose-to-nose with him. "Then we'll come up with another trick. Do you want **to take that risk**? I'm not sure I'd advise that."

The Phantom Ninja gave a slight bow.

"Enjoy the battles to come," he said to the ninja. "Tell Sensei Wu I will leave the tea I owe him in the usual spot . . . and you'll find your gear about one hundred yards behind you in the woods. Farewell!"

With that, the Phantom Ninja vanished into the woods. Kai looked like he wanted to go after him, but Cole stopped him with a look.

"Whoever he is, whatever reason he did what he did, maybe he taught us all a lesson," said Cole. "Come on, let's gather our gear . . . and then we have skeletons to track down. Right?"

Zane, Kai, and Jay looked at one another, and then at Cole. "Right!" they said together. And with that, they set off, knowing that no matter what challenge awaited them, Cole was the best leader to guide them.